THE GHOST IN THE MIRROR

MARCIA CHAMBERS KRUCHTEN

*digital cover illustration
by Michael Petty*

For Mike

∭PAGES™

Fourth printing by Willowisp Press 1996.

Published by Willowisp Press
801 94th Avenue North, St. Petersburg, Florida 33702

Printed in the United States of America

4 6 8 10 9 7 5

ISBN 0-87406-815-0

One

I should have known all along that things weren't what they seemed to be. The house tried to tell me, but I wouldn't listen. I was too wrapped up in my own problems to see. And the ghost was there all the time, waiting for me. . . .

It all started the day we moved. Dark clouds chased each other across the sky. Each gust of rain only made the day more gloomy. I remember the way the rain beat against the car window. Every hour Mom drove took me farther from everything I wanted. Every hour brought me closer to a town I'd never seen before . . . a house I wouldn't belong in.

The twins were cranky, and I was tired of listening to them. I watched a streak of water race into another one on the glass, and sighed.

"You're awfully quiet, Jenny," Mom said, looking at me in the rearview mirror. I didn't answer.

"It won't be long now," Dad offered. He looked pale. The doctors had said his heart surgery would fix everything. But it hadn't happened like that. If he didn't get stronger pretty soon, he might have to have more surgery. Mom told me we'd have to wait and see. But I couldn't help worrying.

"There's the school," Dad said, pointing. "Our house is just around the corner."

"And this is the downtown section," Mom added. We were past the street filled with lighted stores before I could see much. It didn't look too exciting.

"There," Dad said. "That's the driveway."

Mom turned the car into a dark drive overhung with old, straggling trees. At the end of the driveway sat a tall, gaunt house. A light moved and glimmered in an upstairs window.

"Who's in there?" I cried, startled.

"What?" Dad asked, turning to look at me.

"There's a light in that window," I insisted.

Dad twisted back around in the seat. "Don't be silly, Jenny," he said. "You've seen the reflection of the streetlight. Pull in there, at the side of the house," he told Mom.

I sank back into the seat, frowning. I knew what I'd seen, but the light wasn't there any more. I shrugged and climbed out of the car. Sally, my big sister, and the boys were already out. Mom ran around the car to help Dad.

I knew right away the house was different. It was more than just that it was old and run-down. It was a feeling I had . . . a feeling that the house held secrets. I stared at it in the dusk and shivered. Its gray paint was peeling, and overgrown shrubs reached wildly into the porch.

It had stopped raining. I could hear the bushes dripping on the wooden floor boards of the porch. I couldn't catch my breath for a moment. The drops struck the wood with a sound like my own heart beating. I felt dizzy and a little scared.

"This is it?" I blurted. I wasn't frightened any more. I was angry instead. I couldn't believe Mom and Dad would do this to me. I knew times were tough, but did that mean we had to live in a dump?

"Be thankful we have a place to go to, Jenny Morgan," Mom said. Her voice was sharp.

I bit my lip and stared at the crack in the sidewalk. I tried not to think. If I stopped to remember what I left behind, I'd cry. "It looks like a haunted house," I muttered resentfully.

"It needs paint," Dad told me, "that's all." He sat down hard on the bottom step. Mother caught her breath, and her chin went up. I could see she was trying not to worry Dad. After all he'd been through, he needed to rest. He didn't need to hear my dumb mouth making things worse.

Daniel and David had already rushed into the house. The lawyer said he had switched on the electricity, and he had. The twins were turning on lights in one room after another. This was just one big adventure to them. If I were six years old, maybe I'd feel that way, too.

"Sally," Mom sighed, "go after them, will you?" She turned to Dad. "Bless Uncle Henry," she said. "This will be a fine home with a little paint and work." She helped Dad up the steps. I guess they'd forgotten about me, but that was okay. I didn't feel like talking anyway.

I hauled my suitcase out of the trunk of the car. What difference did it make if I liked the house or not? Like Mom said, we had no choice. If Great-uncle Henry hadn't left the house to Dad, we'd have no place to live. Dad hadn't worked for a long time. We'd been forced to sell our place. There wasn't any point in my thinking about our old home or my old school or the bedroom I'd talked Mom into letting me fix up. I'd had to tell my best friend good-bye. I was sure I wouldn't see her again. So I might as well forget about what I wanted.

I ran up the wooden steps and stopped to look around—not that there was much to see. This was the only ugly house on the block. The others that I could see were neat one-story houses, built close to the street. I wondered what the kids who lived in those houses thought of this old house. Maybe they thought it was haunted, too.

Something rattled and scraped against the porch. I ran into the house shouting for Mom. Then I realized the noise must have been the branches hitting against the porch. I felt pretty stupid. It's a good thing nobody had heard me yelling, I thought. They'd never let me forget it.

The light from the chandelier in the front room made everything glaringly bright. The furniture, what there was of it, was awful. But the moving truck would be here the next day with our own furniture. "It could be worse," I told myself, trying to believe it.

I could hear Mom upstairs fussing at the twins. Sally came floating down the winding staircase. I could tell she was being a movie star again. "What a lovely stairway for a home wedding," Sally sighed.

"Have you lost your mind?" I asked. I was a little loud, I guess, because Dad came into the room frowning at us.

"Don't fight, girls," Dad warned. "Go and

look at the kitchen. It's just like it was when I was a boy. The wood stove's still there. Think of it!"

Sally started complaining that she was too tired, and I ignored her. Dad looked cheery. I figured anything that made him feel better had to be good. I went to look at the kitchen like he had asked, but it was bad. It was big and cobwebby. The floor was covered with chipped linoleum. There was an old clunky-looking table in the middle of the room. I wrote my name in the dust on it and went off to find Mom.

I picked up my suitcase in the hall and started up the stairs. Sally, of course, had disappeared. I saw Dad stretched out in an old chair. Maybe he'd be happy here, I thought. He had told us so often how he used to visit his Uncle Henry in the summers.

I wasn't thinking about much when I stopped on the landing to look out an oval window. I knew the glass in the window was old. Antiques were Dad's hobby. He'd told me how they used to make glass. It made things look curved around the edges. And the little bubbles in the glass made the backyard look strange.

It was almost dark, but there was enough daylight left to show that the yard needed a lot of work. A long sidewalk led to the back of the lot. There, a tree with crooked branches stood against the sky. I had begun to turn away when I saw a girl in the yard. I breathed on the glass and rubbed a clean spot to look through.

As I pressed my face to the window, the girl lifted her head. She turned her pale face toward my window. I stared at her. A dull roaring began to sound in my head, and my heart thudded in my chest. I felt cold and sick. I grabbed at the window ledge to steady myself. I thought I heard a voice calling my name. *Jenn-ee . . . Jenn-ee . . .*

I must have cried out. The next thing I knew, I was lying on the landing with Mom's worried face hovering over me. She had my wrist, taking my pulse.

"Carrie? What happened?" Dad panted, pulling himself up the stairs by the railing.

"Mom? Mom?" It was the twins, hanging over the upstairs banisters. "Did Jenny fall?"

"What did happen?" Mom asked me.

I couldn't tell her what I didn't know myself. Did I faint? I wondered. I'd never fainted before.

"She wouldn't eat all day," Sally said, running down the stairs toward us.

"She's had too much excitement," Mom decided. "Boys, go back to bed. Sally, go make

Jenny a sandwich. And get her a glass of water. Look in the cooler. There should be some peanut butter you can use. Go on," Mom insisted. Sally flew toward the kitchen.

"Carl, she's all right," Mom went on firmly. "Jenny, I've had enough of your pouting. You'll eat a sandwich and go to bed. I want you to get up tomorrow with a better attitude. Do you hear me?"

"Carrie," Dad protested, but Mom wouldn't hear him.

"If she'd eaten something today, we wouldn't have this now," she told Dad.

"It was just that I was looking at the girl," I began, indignantly. I hadn't fainted because I was hungry. It wasn't fair of Mom to blame me because I hadn't had any appetite all day. "There was a girl in the backyard, and I was just looking at her."

"I don't want to hear any more, Jenny," Mom said. She was using her no-nonsense nurse's voice. I knew what that meant. She had finished talking, and that was that.

Sally shoved the sandwich at me. "Eat it and go to bed," she ordered, and went past me up the stairs.

"You're not my mother," I snapped at her.

"Jenny," Dad groaned.

"I'm eating, I'm eating," I cried, taking a big

bite of sandwich. Why was everybody picking on me?

"It's time for bed, everyone," Mom said loudly.

I finished the sandwich and shrugged. Then I went on upstairs. The whole day had been a mess. All I wanted to do was go to sleep. Besides, I still felt kind of cold. Burrowing under blankets sounded good to me. I really didn't think I'd fainted from hunger, but Mom ought to know. She's a nurse, after all. Maybe I'm catching the flu or something, I thought. I was so tired my feet dragged on the wide pine floorboards.

There were two beds in the front bedroom. Sally had picked her bed and was already asleep. I found my pajamas wadded up in the bottom of my suitcase. I put them on and climbed between the sheets. They smelled musty, and the mattress was hard.

I heard Mom and Dad settle into bed across the hall. I just lay there, thinking. A car came down the street. The headlights drew a ghostly glow that moved slowly across my ceiling and down the wall. When the light was gone, I suddenly realized how black the shadows were in the corners. I found myself watching the shadows as if something might creep out of one of them.

The house creaked and popped, and I jerked upright in bed. "Stupid," I said to myself, flouncing back under the covers. "Old houses make noises. I know that."

I stuck the pillow over my head, thinking about that girl in our backyard. What had she been doing there, anyway? Maybe she lived close by and used our yard for a shortcut or something.

I began worrying about making friends in a new school. Finally I went to sleep, remembering vaguely that someone had been calling my name just before I'd fainted. There was something about that I wanted to remember, but I couldn't think what it was.

Two

I woke the next morning to the smell of bacon drifting up the stairs. Mom knew how to get me out of bed, all right. Sunlight poured in the windows as I rummaged in my suitcase. I found a clean sweatshirt and dressed quickly. Sally's unmade bed was empty. That meant I must have slept late. Usually I'm the first one up after Mom. I was still tired, though. I'd had strange dreams all night. Most of them had been about a little animal that snarled through sharp white teeth.

The twins nearly knocked me down as they raced up the stairs. They were noisy, as usual. I hoped they weren't going to giggle like that all day.

I stopped on the landing to look out the oval window. I don't know what I expected to see. There was nothing there but a neglected yard. There were a lot of shrubs—rosebushes, too—

that needed trimming. The grass had been let go for so long that it was a disaster. Somebody needed to mow it right away, and that meant me. Sally never wants to ruin her nail-polish doing such things. I really like mowing, so that was okay with me.

"When's breakfast?" I demanded as I hit the kitchen. Mom was pulling food out of the cooler. She had both hands full of eggs. The cobwebs had been swept from the ceiling, and the table had been scrubbed, too. There was a fire in the wood stove. I backed up to it, feeling the warmth through my snug denim jeans.

"I'll scramble these. That's quicker," Mom said. Dad grinned at her from his chair. "You always did like my scrambled eggs, Carl," she told him, smiling.

"Where's Sally?" I asked, grabbing a piece of toast from a plate.

"Sally's gone to the market," Dad told me. "We needed more bread, and milk."

"If you'd been up, sleepy-head, you could have gone with her," Mom said. "You need to start meeting people here."

I made a face. "Why would I want to meet some dumb people in a grocery store?" I scoffed. "Besides, the yard's a mess. When the moving van gets here, I want to get the lawn mower out right away. It's a good thing you've

14

got me," I bragged. I thought it was about time someone realized I did things for the family, too.

From the look on Dad's face, I wished I hadn't said it. I knew he wanted to mow himself. But he couldn't, not yet anyway. A buzzer sounded in the room, and I jumped.

"That's the back doorbell," Dad said.

I ran to open the door. A boy stood there, grinning.

"Hi," he said. "I'm Paul Grover. If you want to have the newspaper delivered, I'm your man." He pulled off his baseball cap, waiting for an answer. He had the reddest hair I'd ever seen and freckles to go with it.

"Can you start right away?" Dad asked from behind me. "I know Uncle Henry liked getting the paper. And we need to begin learning about our new town."

"Sure thing," the boy nodded. "I'll collect every Saturday, if that's all right? I'll start you today. Say," he said to me, "what grade will you be in this fall?"

I was so surprised that I couldn't think for a minute. "Oh," I stammered. "Sixth. I mean, I just finished the sixth. I'll be in junior high, I guess."

"I'll be in the seventh grade myself," Paul said. "Do you have any brothers and sisters?"

I nodded. "I have an older sister, Sally.

15

She'll be a junior in high school. And I have twin brothers who'll be in the first grade."

"Well, I just live down there," he said, pointing across the yard. "I live in the last house on this block."

"Oh," I said.

"See you around." He nodded and jumped on his bike, whirling away. I wished I'd asked him if he had a sister and if he knew the girl I'd seen in our backyard last night.

"Who was that?" Mom called.

"Paperboy," Dad answered. "Jenny, get another chair from the dining room, please."

"His name's Paul Grover," I grumbled. Couldn't Dad remember a name for five minutes? "He's going to be in my class." I started to carry in a chair.

Sally came flying through the back door. "Mom! Dad! Guess what?" She plopped two sacks on the table, looking like she'd won a million dollars or something. That usually meant she'd met a cute boy.

"Well, what?" I asked rudely. Sometimes Sally got on my nerves.

"I've got a job," Sally cried.

"Oh, honey, that's great," Mom said, hugging her.

"Where?" Dad asked. He looked surprised and a little grim.

"The market down the street," Sally said. She laughed. "They want me to start right away. After school starts, I can work evenings and Saturdays. I can save for college, Dad. Just think!"

"Well, I don't know, Sally," Dad began.

I dropped my chair. It made a lot of noise. I'd meant for it to. Everybody stared at me.

"You can't do that," I said.

Sally's eyebrows rose. I hated that. "Why not?" she cried.

"You're supposed to watch Daniel and David while Mom works, that's why. How are you supposed to do that if you're working, too?"

"Listen, you can watch the twins," Sally told me, turning red. "You've got nothing better to do."

The twins fell through the door. I knew they were somewhere listening. They'd been too quiet. Well, this time they'd overheard something they hadn't wanted to hear.

"Mom, do I have to mind Jenny? She's not old enough!" Daniel shrieked.

David started whining, but Mom ignored it. Then they started bothering Dad about it, and Mom put her foot down.

"I'll not hear another word," Mom said. "Eat your breakfast, all of you."

"I already told them I'd take the job," Sally

pleaded. "I'm supposed to start tomorrow."

"Your father and I will discuss it," Mom said, looking tired.

"I'm not baby-sitting," I said loudly. "That's flat. I've got enough trouble." I couldn't believe Sally thought she could push that off on me! Well, she could just think again.

"Jenny, that's enough," Mom scolded. "I told you yesterday about your attitude, remember?"

I was breathing hard and trying not to cry. I looked at the ratty linoleum on the floor. It looked like I felt.

I left the kitchen and ran upstairs. Somebody was knocking on the front door. Then the doorbell rang. Let dear little Sally answer it, I thought. I ran through the upper hall and flung myself across the bed. Was this the way things were going to be in this ugly old house?

There were voices in the hall below, not that I cared. I clutched a pillow and tried to think about something pleasant. But it didn't work. Before I knew it, I was wiping my eyes and trying not to make any noise crying. I couldn't understand why Mom was picking on me.

The big room darkened as if a cloud had passed between the window and the sun. The voices in the downstairs hall faded away. I heard a small sound close by, and then another. It was like a muffled sob.

Everybody but me was downstairs. What could that be? I wondered. I sat up to listen. The bedroom was silent, and then I heard it again. It came from outside the room. Curious, I swung my legs off the bed and went to look.

The empty hall was dim and shadowed. I looked in the next room where the twins had slept. It was empty, too. But the sound came again, closer this time.

I walked across the hall to the third bedroom. Mom's robe was lying over the foot of the bed. Nobody was there either. I wandered back into the hall. A whisper hung in the air. *Over here . . .* it sighed.

I scowled at the barely open bathroom door. Sally had to be in there trying to scare me. "Big deal," I muttered. I turned away and then realized there was a door I'd missed. It was beyond the room I'd just left, and a shadow lay across it. I started toward the door. Someone giggled behind me. I whirled, but nobody was there. "Knock it off, Sally," I threatened.

I turned the knob and found a small room full of sunlight. It had four windows that overlooked the backyard. There was a big, old tree just outside. The tree was so close to the house that a branch brushed against one of the windows. Leaf shadows danced across the wall. A narrow bed and a wooden wardrobe filled up the room. I loved the bed. It was iron, and the frame was all curling leaves and roses.

I plopped down on the bed. It was just my size. It felt like it was practically made for me. Then I jumped up and opened the doors to the wardrobe. One whole side was filled with empty drawers. The other side was for hanging clothes. It was empty except for an oval mirror. The mirror had a wooden frame that was carved with roses, just like the bed. It had been painted white, too, but was badly chipped. My fingers traced the carved pattern slowly.

"So there you are!"

I looked toward the door, expecting Sally, but it was Mom.

"What a sweet room this is!" Mom went on. "I didn't realize it was here."

"Mom, may I have it?" I begged. "I need a room of my own." I turned the old mirror around in my hands. It had a strong wire fastened to the back. There was a nail in the wall, and I hung the mirror on it. I couldn't believe it. It was just the right height for me.

"Even the mirror fits me," I said. "See, Mom?"

"Jenny, this old wallpaper is still good," Mom marveled. She hadn't even heard me. "See these delicate yellow flowers? Look at the way the sunlight's faded them? It's charming."

"I need this room," I insisted, raising my voice. "There's only one closet in the front bedroom, and Sally's stuff will fill it up. You know that."

"Will your old curtains fit in here?" Mom wondered. "Oh, Jenny. This room is really right for you."

I knew Sally was hiding close by, because I heard her giggle. At least, I thought I did. "Sally can't have this room," I said loudly. "She'll want it because I do. You know she will."

Mom grinned. "I just told you this room is yours," she said.

Dad shouted up to tell us the moving van had arrived. Mom ran down the stairs, and I stood in my little bedroom hugging myself. It was warm and quiet. I could hear dimly the sound of doors slamming downstairs.

"This is my room," I told myself, ". . . all mine."

The words seemed to echo in the stillness.

My roo-oom . . . my roo-oom . . . sighed all around me.

"Sally?" I waited, but there was no other sound. I shrugged. It was just like Sally to pull a trick like that to scare me.

"Well, it won't work, Sally. I don't believe in ghosts," I said, starting for the stairs. Halfway down, I found myself humming an odd little tune. At first I couldn't remember where I'd heard it, and then I stopped humming. I knew I'd never heard that song before.

I shivered and rushed down the rest of the steps to find Mom.

Three

IT was wild in the hall. There was a lot of confusion, and the twins were everywhere. People were tramping in and out with boxes and furniture. Mom was busy telling the men where to put everything. I dodged past the couch being carried in and ran to the kitchen. I grabbed a big slab of chocolate cake that hadn't been there before. I guessed a neighbor must have brought it in. I took the cake and a glass of milk to a corner of the front porch. I figured Sally could watch the twins. She'd already had her breakfast.

It had been cool earlier that morning. But the sun was already burning off the summer fog. The air was fresh and clean—not at all like the air had been in the city where we'd lived before. I took a deep breath, and then another. The chocolate cake was great. I popped the last bite into my mouth and wadded up my napkin. The song I'd been humming on the stairs kept running through my mind. I didn't want to hear it. I jumped up and ran off the porch.

The moving men were still carrying things into the house. I went around the truck to the backyard. The lawnmower was sitting by the back door. There was a building that looked like a garage at the back of the lot. I wheeled the mower toward it. I figured the garage would be a good place to store the mower until I could use it.

It wasn't a garage, and it was locked. I mean, it was definitely locked. There was a padlock on the door. I looked in one of the little windows. The glass was thick with dust, but I could see there was a lot of old furniture inside. I groaned. There wasn't enough room left in there to store a rake. Why had Dad's Uncle Henry filled up a perfectly good building with junk? Now we'd have to pay to have it hauled away.

I heard the moving van pull out of the driveway. When I turned to watch them leave, I saw Sally running across the lawn toward me.

"Where have you been hiding?" Sally snapped. "There's a lot of work to do, you know." She pushed her long hair back from her face, scowling.

I ignored Sally's question. I jerked my head at the building. "It's full of trash. I can't get the mower in there, and there's no garage."

Sally stood on tiptoe and peered in a window. "Antiques!" she gasped. "It's full of antiques, Jenny!"

"Oh, come on," I said. "Junk's junk. You always have to be so fancy."

"What's all this?" Dad asked.

I hadn't seen him coming, and I looked at him, worried. He was pale. He really ought to be resting, I thought.

"The shed is full of junk that Sally calls antiques," I told him. "What a mess!"

"Well." Dad started fishing in his pockets. He found an enormous key and fiddled with the padlock. At last it clicked open. He pushed the door in far enough to squeeze through. He didn't say anything, but he had a strange look on his face.

"What is it, Dad?" I asked, pulling at his arm. "Don't you think you'd better go to the house?"

"Let me see," Sally cried, pushing in past him.

"Jenny, this isn't a shed. It's a small barn," Dad said. "And it's full of old furniture. They're not antiques, but they're solid and well-built." He stopped to catch his breath.

25

"Henry told me once he had a surprise legacy for me. I guess this is what he meant."

"What do you mean?" Sally asked.

"Well, if these pieces were cleaned up. . . . They'll have to be refinished and reglued, of course. People are buying old furniture now."

"Who could fix them up, though?" I argued. "You're talking about a lot of work, Dad. You can't do it."

Dad looked at me. "I'm stronger every day, Jenny," he said.

"Why did he store these things here?" Sally asked. "The house was almost empty when we got here. He could have used this furniture in the house."

Dad grinned. "You'd have to have known my uncle," he said. "He believed all a man needed was a bed, a table, and one chair. He said furniture got in his way."

Sally held up a blue and white pitcher. It was about eight inches tall. It looked very old and had fine cracks running all over it.

"Be careful with that," Dad warned. "I don't know what it's worth."

I stared at the pitcher. I knew I'd never seen it before. Then why is it so familiar? I wondered. I knew before looking that there was a tiny crown over an "H" on the bottom. And I was right. "Dad . . . " I began, puzzled.

"Sally?" It was Mom, calling from the back door. "Where are the boys? I can't find them in here."

"Oh, no," Sally gasped. "I told them we'd go for a walk."

"I hope they didn't go for a walk by themselves," I said. "Weren't you supposed to be baby-sitting?"

"That's enough, Jenny," Dad sighed. He pulled a straight-backed chair through the door and sat down on it. "I'll sit here in the sun for a bit," he said. "You and Sally go find the boys."

I hesitated, watching him. "Don't you think you ought to go back to the house?" I asked.

"Don't you think you ought to look for the twins?" he replied. He waved me away.

Sally was running toward the school and the playground. I decided to look downtown. It was just a couple of blocks away. If I knew the twins, they'd go where the action was. That meant food.

"They've probably talked someone into buying them ice cream cones," I grumbled, walking fast.

It only took about five minutes to get to Main Street. I started looking in each shop I thought they might be in. I was really starting to get worried by the time I got to the dime store. But there they were. A girl with a furious face was shaking David. He was screeching, and Daniel was busy kicking the girl in the shins. I raced toward them.

"You stop that," I cried. Red-faced, the girl gave David a final shake. "I told you to take your hands off my brother," I shouted. I pulled David away from her and snatched up Daniel's hand.

"These brats came in here without any money and looked at everything in the store," the girl fumed. "If they can't buy, you ought to keep them at home." Daniel aimed another kick at the girl, and I knew how he felt.

"Kim Blair!" An older man appeared at the girl's elbow, looking astonished. "Apologize to these customers at once!"

"What?" the girl cried. "But, Mr. Bailey . . . "

"Kim?" he repeated, frowning.

"I'm sorry," the girl mumbled. But you could tell she wasn't.

"Please, young lady, accept our apologies," the man told me. "Our customers come first at Bailey's. They always have." He looked at the girl. "Kim seems to have forgotten that just now."

"Oh!" the girl gasped, and flounced away.

"You must be Henry Morgan's great-niece," Mr. Bailey said. "The family resemblance is remarkable. I hope your father's better."

"How did you know?" I blurted, surprised.

Mr. Bailey chuckled. "Henry was my good friend. He brought your father in here with him when your father was no bigger than these boys. I'm glad your family didn't sell the house to Leonard Fox. Your father will get better here. You'll see. Say, you don't need a part-time job, do you?"

I was really sorry to have to tell him no. I had the feeling I'd be stuck with watching the twins, though it wasn't settled yet.

"Maybe later," Mr. Bailey told me. "Keep us in mind, will you?"

I told him I would, and shoved the boys out of the store. Kim Blair glared at me from the window, but I ignored her. Who did she think she was, anyway?

"She smacked me," David whined.

"Daniel kicked her in the shins, too," I said. "Why did you run off, anyway? This is no way to make friends in a new town. You guys are going to have to do better, you know. You can't worry Mom and Dad like that."

I hurried the twins home and turned them over to Mom. Then I ran upstairs to look at my room again. Dad was standing in the doorway.

"Don't you like this room?" I asked.

29

"I always have, Jenny. So did Uncle Henry," Dad said, looking around. "It's always been like it is now."

"What do you mean?"

"This room . . . Uncle Henry wouldn't change the wallpaper or use it for a guest bedroom," Dad told me. "This was his mother's room when she was a girl. Henry tried to keep it pretty much as she left it."

Dad's words gave me a spooky feeling. "That's really strange," I said slowly.

"Why? Henry's mother loved this room. He had plenty of room in the rest of the house." Dad shrugged. "Henry would have been glad for you to use it."

"What makes you say that?" I asked.

"You were named for Uncle Henry's mother. Surely you know that. She was your great-grandmother."

"Oh," I said. I knew Jenny was an old family name, but I hadn't realized whose name it was.

"Yes, we'll have another Jenny in Jenny's room. It seems right somehow," Dad said. He tousled my hair. "Listen, we'll get some white paint. The furniture needs painting in here." He looked thoughtful. "You'll be lucky in this room," he said with a nod.

"I hope so," I said doubtfully. "Say, Dad, when I found the twins, they were in Bailey's dime store. I talked to Mr. Bailey. He said he was glad you hadn't sold this house to Leonard something . . . Leonard Fox, I think he said. Who's that? I didn't hear anything about selling the house."

Dad grimaced. "We're not selling. We certainly wouldn't sell to Lenny Fox. He's the lawyer who handled the will. Remember?"

"You don't like him?" I asked.

"I didn't say that," Dad answered. "I have no reason to dislike him. But he wants this house too badly. Henry said once Lenny Fox was all right, for a lawyer." He laughed. "No, this is our home, and we'll keep it. You'll make friends before long. We all will."

"Sure, Dad," I said. But I wasn't sure at all. So far Kim Blair was the only girl I'd met, and I didn't like her. I started down the stairs, worrying again about making friends. School was only a month away.

I glanced out the oval window as I reached the landing. That girl was in our backyard again. She was holding an armful of flowers and was walking toward the house. Pleased, I rushed downstairs and out the back door to meet her. But when I got there, the yard was empty. She was gone.

Disappointed, I went back into the house. I'd hoped the girl had come to make friends.

But I guessed she had just been taking a shortcut, after all.

I rummaged through a box labeled "Shoes" and found my grass-stained sneakers. It was time to mow the lawn. At least I'm good at that, I thought.

Four

SALLY took the job at the market, of course. Just as I thought, I got stuck with baby-sitting the twins. But since Mom's new job wouldn't start for another week, I had time to fix up my room first.

Mom began putting the house in order. She washed windows and woodwork, put up curtains, and began waxing floors. Dad fixed the meals—mostly sandwiches. Mom did the cleaning. I meant to help her. I really did. But I couldn't. As soon as I finished one thing in my room, I found another that needed doing.

First, I painted the furniture. Then I took up the paint-spattered newspapers from the floor. The freshly painted furniture made the floor look dull, so I waxed it until it shone. Then I cleaned and waxed the woodwork. I couldn't seem to stop. The twins tried to help, but I chased them out. They were more a nuisance than a help. Besides, I had to do it myself.

Mom told me to use my old curtains, but I couldn't. They were okay, but they were wrong for this room. It needed plain white curtains. I took a white sheet from the linen closet and cut it up. Mom got mad, but Dad told her to leave me alone. I guess they had a big fight about it, but it didn't seem important. The only thing that mattered to me was finishing the room. Somehow, I knew I couldn't move in until the room was done—that it wouldn't be mine until then.

Sally looked in my door late one afternoon and frowned at me. I'd hardly seen her all week, but I hadn't missed her.

"Why are you wasting time with that?" she argued. "Your old curtains would've been okay. You ought to forget that and go help Mom. You could be watching the boys, you know. I have a job. I can't do it."

I didn't answer her. I was sitting cross-legged on my bed, sewing. I didn't have time to waste. I had to get the curtains done.

"Mom's ripping up the linoleum in the kitchen," Sally said, wandering into my room. "She says she's going to paint the floorboards blue or something. It'll look better than that horrible linoleum. How do you stand it in here? This room is at least twenty degrees hotter than the rest of the house." She picked up the blue pitcher I'd taken from the barn, turning it over in her hands.

"Put that back, please. It's mine," I said coldly.

"Yours?" Sally's brows lifted. "Since when?"

"It's always been mine," I said, biting the thread. "There." I shook out the panel I'd just finished.

"You're weird, Jenny. Do you know that?" Sally said, staring at me.

I began to push a curtain rod through the material. It didn't matter what Sally thought. All that mattered was the room. I had to get it done. I hung all the curtains carefully and stepped back to look at them. I didn't notice when Sally left.

I looked around the room. Something wasn't quite right. Something was missing. I stood very still, listening. And then it came to me. There should be a table in the corner—a small oak table, with one drawer and slender legs.

I went downstairs. Mom had most of the linoleum pulled up from the kitchen floor. I stepped over it. Then I took the barn key from the nail on the back porch. I went to the barn and started moving furniture. Dad had followed me. He stood watching as I pulled the table out.

"Jenny," he began, looking at me oddly.

"I need this table," I said. "It's mine."

"You've spent the whole week upstairs," Dad told me. "Is there anything wrong?"

"I'm almost done," I said, picking up the table.

I carried the table back through the house. Mom said something to me, but I didn't listen. I took the table to my room and began to polish it. I rubbed it furiously. The little table gleamed when I stopped.

I'd been right. The table looked as if it had always been in that corner. I set the blue pitcher on top and smiled. I was pleased. The room was complete now. Now it was mine.

I was more tired than I'd ever been in my life. And I realized suddenly that I was starving. I looked at my room with satisfaction and turned to go downstairs.

But before I could take a step, the air began to fill with warm fragrance. I could have been standing in a rose garden on a hot June day. I caught my breath. A voice murmured through the deep hush that held the room. I couldn't make out the words. Dazed, I reached to hold the door frame with both hands. I felt sleepy, and safe . . . so safe. My head began to droop.

The sweet scent left as suddenly as it had come. The whispering voice was silent. There was nothing but my spotless room in the sunlight. I stared at the pitcher on my table. Something very strange had just happened.

I let go of the door frame. I knew I couldn't tell anyone about this. They'd never understand. I didn't understand either, but I knew what had happened was important to me. "This will have to be my secret," I told myself. Sally would be sure I was cracking up if she heard this story.

I stepped into the hall, shivering. Sally had been right about one thing. The rest of the house was cooler than my room. It was funny that I'd never noticed. I guess I'd been too busy. Well, I could move into my room now, I thought as I went down the stairs. I'd sleep in there tonight. There'd be no more sharing with Sally.

* * * * *

I couldn't believe the difference in the house. Mom must have worked like a whirlwind to get it all done. Our own furniture sat comfortably in the big living room. Familiar curtains framed the sparkling windows. Everything seemed to blend in. It looked like a home now, welcoming and well-used. With Dad's watercolors up on the walls, even the faded wallpaper looked brighter.

"Hi, Jen." Dad stood in the dining room by the fireplace, looking at an old clock on the mantel. He closed the glass over the clock face and laid a key down beside the clock. "Are you ready to come back to the real world now?" he asked.

"What do you mean?" Does he know about my room? I wondered. When he answered, I knew he didn't.

"Well, we've not seen much of you lately," Dad said. "Of course I realize it's important to you to have your own room. But I began to wonder if we'd lost you somewhere." He turned his attention back to the clock.

"Where did the clock come from?" I questioned, going toward it.

Dad shook his head. "That's what I mean, Jenny. You should know it's been sitting right here. It was here when we moved in. Where have you been?"

"It should be running," I said slowly.

Dad shrugged. "I set the face and wound both the time and the strike. I guess I'll have to take the back off now to start the weight swinging." He reached for the clock.

"No. Here," I said. My hand went to the right side of the clock's base. I tipped it up and back down quickly—just a little, just an inch or so. The clock began to tick with a steady, comforting rhythm. "It belongs here, on this mantel," I said, smiling.

"How did you know to do that?" Dad asked.

"It's a shy little clock," I said. "If you bother it much, it won't run."

A strange look came over Dad's face. I laughed. "Come on, Dad," I said. "You must have told me that."

Dad looked at me intently. "No, Jenny," he replied. "I couldn't have told you that. I didn't know it."

"Well, I read it somewhere then," I said impatiently. "What difference does it make? What's for supper? I could eat a horse," I groaned.

I left Dad looking at the clock and went to the kitchen. The delicious aroma of chocolate met me. The twins were licking the leftover batter. Daniel had the bowl, and David the beaters. I swiped a glob of batter from the bowl with my finger, and Daniel shrieked.

"When I get really old, I'm going to eat nothing but chocolate," I sighed.

"When you get really old, you'll have a bad complexion, then," Mom said. "Are you done playing with that bedroom? Because if you are, I can use some help." She stopped to wipe her face with a paper towel. Her cheeks were flushed, and she looked pretty tired.

"Are you okay, Mom?" I asked, concerned.

"Jenny, it's hot! Or haven't you noticed? Set the table, please. Boys, go wash up. You've got chocolate all over you."

I felt guilty that I'd left Mom with everything to do. "Has Sally helped any this week? She doesn't work at the store all the time," I argued, trying to make myself feel better. I went to the cabinet to get the plates.

"She's been putting in extra hours. The manager has the flu," Mom said, giving me a sharp glance. "If you hadn't been so wrapped up in your room, you'd know that." Mom paused. Then she got that determined look and went on. "I don't like the word 'obsession,' Jenny," she told me. "But I don't like what's been going on with you this week. It's not healthy to devote all your time to that room."

I felt my face get hot. "Okay, okay," I muttered. What's wrong with everybody, anyway? I wondered. I began to set the table, not looking at Mom.

"Isn't it time for dinner yet?" Sally asked, coming through the door. Then she saw me. "Well guess who decided to join us? You mean you actually left your room?"

I looked at her blankly.

"Earth to Jenny. Come in, Jenny."

40

"Knock it off, Sally," I threatened.

Mom took the cake out of the oven. "Jenny, there's egg salad in the refrigerator. Sally, get the ice cubes. I want you two to stop fighting, I don't want this going on while I'm at work."

"Your job doesn't start until Monday," I said.

"That's tomorrow," Sally told me.

"Really?" I was astonished. It couldn't be Sunday already. I saw Mom watching me. "Hey, I know that," I said quickly. "I was only kidding."

"Sure," Sally drawled.

"I'm starving," I said loudly. I said it to change the subject, but it was true.

As I ate my way through supper, I could tell Mom was starting to relax. She wasn't watching me with that funny look any more.

By the time I'd had two pieces of cake, everything was back to normal.

I volunteered to do the dishes by myself. After Mom's job started tomorrow, I wouldn't be spending much more time alone. I'd be running after the twins instead. That should make Mom happy. Anyway, I'd have the nights to myself. I couldn't wait to sleep in my room. I began humming that odd little tune again. I admired the glass I'd just polished dry. Smiling, I reached for another.

41

Five

MOM had to work day shift for a week before going on the three-to-eleven evening shift. Things seemed to settle down pretty well by the end of that week. After one day of chasing the boys all over the neighborhood, I dug out their swim trunks. That worked so well that I started taking them to the pool every morning. When they were good and tired, I would take them home for a sandwich and check on Dad. Then we went back to the pool. By the time we got back home again each afternoon, Mom was there. It kept Daniel and David busy, and I got to work on my tan. If I had to baby-sit, I might as well make the best of it.

I moved into my own room. I loved being alone in it. There hadn't been any more flower scent or whispering. But the feeling of being safe there had stayed. Each night I slept deep and dreamlessly.

Dad had claimed the enclosed back porch for his workshop. He'd begun refinishing an old chest of drawers. Mom wasn't sure if he should be trying it, but he insisted. He'd work a while and then rest. By the end of the week, even Mom was impressed with his progress. The chest had been stripped of its old blue paint, and Dad was excited. He said it was a good piece of furniture. If it made him happy, I guessed it was worth the mess he made.

I'd begun worrying about making friends again. Everybody seemed to show up at the pool with a friend or in a group. I felt left out. I just watched the twins and pretended I didn't care. But I did. I wondered if I'd ever fit in here.

The only person I'd found to talk to was Paul Grover. I asked him if he knew the girl I'd seen in our yard. He shook his head. He said it didn't sound like anybody he knew.

I was sitting on the side of the pool on Saturday, rubbing lotion on my legs, when Paul pulled himself out of the pool beside me.

"How's it going?" he puffed, wiping his eyes.

"Look around," I said, waving my hand. "Here I sit all by myself like I've been doing all week. Maybe it'll be different when school starts."

Paul shrugged. "Hey," he said. "Somebody

has to make the first move. Maybe the kids think you're stuck up. You don't even try to talk to them."

"How can I?" I replied, irritated. I thought he'd understand, but I could tell he didn't. "I don't know anybody to talk to."

"You talk to me," he remarked. "It's not such a big deal."

"Maybe not to you . . . ," I began, hurt, but Paul interrupted me.

"Daniel's headed for deep water," he said, pointing.

I jumped up and raced around the pool. "Daniel, you come here," I shouted over the noisy swimmers' heads. He didn't, so I went in after him. I swam over and grabbed his arm. "If you're not going to mind me," I told him, "we're going home, right now!"

"Aw, Mother," a voice whined. I looked up, surprised. There was Kim Blair a couple of yards away. I knew from the smirk on her face that the voice I'd heard belonged to her. The two girls bobbing in the water with her were giggling like crazy. I glared at them and then got Daniel out of the pool. I hoped Paul heard what Kim said. Maybe he'd know what I meant, then.

I headed both the boys toward home. When we turned into the yard from the alley, I saw

Dad talking to a man by the back door. I sent the boys ahead to change clothes. I draped my towel around me and walked toward Dad and the man.

"Mr. Fox, this is my daughter, Jenny," Dad said. "This is Uncle Henry's lawyer, Jen."

A wave of dislike shook me as I stared at the lawyer. It was so strong that I felt sick. I couldn't even speak.

"He's brought something Uncle Henry left for me," Dad said, looking at the envelope in his hand.

"Perhaps you'd better read that now," Mr. Fox said. Somehow, it sounded like an order.

Dad's eyes narrowed. "Oh, I think it could wait," he said. "I'm sure it's a personal letter to me. It couldn't have anything to do with business. You've already taken care of all that, haven't you?"

The lawyer hesitated, then pursed his lips, blinking. He touched his sharp chin, and his black eyes slid to me. A knot began to grow in my stomach. I was really afraid I might throw up. I moved closer to Dad.

Dad pushed the envelope into his back pocket. "I'll share this letter with my wife," he said firmly. "It would be of no interest to you."

"Very well." Mr. Fox bit the words off. His

face was red, and he looked very angry. He turned away and then turned back to Dad. "My offer to purchase this house still stands, Mr. Morgan," he said. "As you know, I intend to remodel it for offices. You can't keep up a house of this size."

I stepped forward and stared at him. "You are wasting your time here," I said coldly. "This is our home, and it is not for sale. Please leave." It was as if someone else had spoken the words.

The lawyer's eyes glittered. "I don't do business with children," he said softly.

Dad gave me a peculiar look, almost a frown. "Jenny shouldn't have said that. But I agree with her," he said. "We won't sell. I hope I won't have to tell you that again." He didn't even look at Mr. Fox as he spoke. He just kept watching me.

The lawyer turned on his heel and climbed into his car without another word.

I watched him start the car. "And don't come back," I said. "You're not wanted here."

Dad had me by the arm. "Jenny," he said, "what's come over you? Do you realize how rude you've been?"

I started to pull away. "Leonard Fox cannot be trusted," I told him. "Surely you can see that."

Dad's face was stern. I'd never seen him look at me like that before. "Maybe your mother's right," he said. "Maybe we ought to think about counseling for you. You don't even act like yourself any more. It's not good for you, or for any of us. You're part of a family, you know."

It felt like someone had thrown ice water in my face. I was dizzy, and scared. "I'm sorry, Dad. Don't tell Mom about this, please?" I begged. "I won't do it again, honest. I'm sorry I was rude."

"Maybe it was wrong to move here," Dad said. "I can't believe how different you are. You were happier back in the city."

"Carl, what's going on out there?" Mom called.

"Please, Dad, don't tell Mom. I was just . . . pretending to be someone else." It wasn't true, but I had to think of something to take that look off his face. "I won't do it again," I said.

It worked. I could see he was starting to believe it. And then he got mad. That was okay. That was much better than having him think I was cracking up.

I got a short sharp lecture. I didn't care, because Dad had promised he wouldn't tell Mom if I'd try to do better. He'd scared me when he said it might have been wrong to move here. I couldn't leave this place now, not when I had my room. I'll be more careful about what I say, I thought, shivering.

Mom looked out the back door. "What is it, Carl?" she asked again. "Was someone here?"

"Oh, just the lawyer," Dad answered. "He still wants the house." He gave me a warning look, and went in.

I followed Dad into the kitchen. He pulled the letter from his pocket and slit it open.

"The lawyer brought us a letter Uncle Henry left for me," Dad said to Mom. He still looked a little grim as he began to read aloud.

My dear Carl Henry,

When you receive this letter, I'll be gone. You already know that I've left the house to you. Since you loved it so much as a boy, you should have it. I want you to be happy in it. Do you still remember how we used to make up riddles on rainy days when we couldn't take our walks? Well, here's my last riddle for you. If you solve it, it will help you more than you know.

Sunshine chases cloudy skies.
Behind the face the treasure lies.

With my love,
Uncle Henry

"I didn't know your name was Carl Henry," I said, surprised.

"It's not," Dad said, blowing his nose. "It's Carl William. That was just my uncle's name for me."

Mom was reading the letter. "What does it mean?" she asked.

"Behind the face the treasure lies," I repeated. It gave me goose bumps. Or maybe my wet bathing suit did.

"It must refer to all that old furniture in the barn," Dad said. "You know, there's good wood hidden under all that old paint and grime, and it's worth money. I'm sure that's what it means."

Somehow, I was just as sure Dad was wrong. I was going to tell him so, but just then Sally came bouncing in from work.

"I have a date!" she announced.

"Sally, we just moved in," Mom told her firmly. "You don't know anyone well enough here to accept a date."

"Mother!" Sally squealed. "I have to go. I already told him I would!"

"Who is this person?" Dad asked.

"Jim Grover. You know, Paul's brother? He's going away to college in two weeks, and he's just gorgeous."

"Good grief," I said, disgusted. "Is that the

boy who spends all his time washing his car?"

"I'll thank you to shut up," Sally cried.

"That's enough," Dad said loudly. "Now, about this date, Sally . . . "

I aimed my wet towel at the washer before I ran upstairs. I could hear the twins arguing in their room across the hall. I grabbed my bathrobe. It was almost time for supper, but if I hurried I could make it. There was a movie on television I wanted to watch. If I already had my shower, maybe I could talk Mom and Dad into letting me stay up to see it.

I raced through my shower, rubbed my hair partly dry with a towel, and went to my room. I flipped on my blow-dryer and stepped in front of the mirror. I'd been turning the riddle over in my mind. It must mean something, I thought. Uncle Henry wouldn't have wasted a riddle on a bunch of old furniture.

"Behind the face the treasure lies," I murmured.

And then it was like time slowed down and stopped. I couldn't hear the twins any more. The room was muffled in silence. I could feel my heart beating slowly in my chest. I stared at myself in the mirror. But the girl looking back at me wasn't me. It was the girl I'd seen in our backyard.

Her lips formed words. *Don't be afraid,* they

said. But I couldn't hear the words in my ears, only in my head. The room grew suddenly breezy, with the air whirling about me. The girl smiled.

"Who are you?" I whispered hoarsely.

And she was gone.

Six

I could hear the blow-dryer again. I stared at the dryer in my hand and looked from it to the mirror. My reflection looked back at me, pale and big-eyed. I heard the dryer clatter to the floor. What had happened? It hadn't been a dream. I knew that much.

"I'm going to tell Mom!" David shouted. "You're in big trouble, Daniel!"

I turned to see David jump onto my bed. I felt dazed and shaky. It was as if I'd been awakened too fast from a deep sleep. But I hadn't been asleep. Automatically, I scooped the dryer from the floor and turned it off.

"Get off my bed," I told David. "What did you do, Daniel?"

Daniel took his hands from behind his back. He had a fistful of small red roses, already wilting.

"He stole them," David said importantly,

"from the yard of a house down the alley."

"They're for you, Jenny," Daniel said in a small voice, "because that Kim was mean to you at the pool."

"Oh, Daniel," I cried. I gave him a hug, surprising both of us. I took the flowers and buried my nose in them. Then I went to the bathroom and filled my blue pitcher with water. The roses began to perk up as soon as I put them in the pitcher. The scent that came from them was the same fragrance I remembered from before . . . from the day I'd finished fixing up my room. They're just roses, I told myself. All roses smell like roses.

Daniel held up his thumb for me to see. He had jabbed himself with a good-sized thorn.

"Am I really in big trouble, Jenny?" Daniel worried.

"Just don't do it again, okay?" I told him.

"I'm going to tell," David began, but I stopped him.

"Drop it, David. Don't bug Mom with it. He won't do it again." I grinned at Daniel, and he stopped looking worried.

"Supper!" Sally shouted up the stairwell.

"This is our secret, remember?" I told the twins. They nodded, and rushed downstairs. I touched the petals of one of the roses. It was like warm silk. The scent hung about me and

53

began to thicken. I didn't want that. I had too much to think about.

"No," I said loudly. I put my clothes on and walked through the door without looking back.

Something was definitely happening to me, and I didn't like it. I was seeing things that weren't there. I knew Sally couldn't be playing a trick on me. There was no way she could have put that girl's face in my mirror. Besides, Sally had never seen the girl. Sally wouldn't know what she looked like even if she could have faked it.

I stopped on the stairs. I realized I was the only one who'd ever seen the girl in the yard. At least I was the only one I knew about. What if she weren't real? Maybe I do need counseling after all, I thought. I was beginning to be frightened.

I went on downstairs. Had I wanted new friends here so badly that I invented one? I wondered. I knew that could happen with little kids. But I was almost in seventh grade.

I paused by the mantel in the dining room, and stared into the old mirror behind the clock. I looked okay. I felt okay, except that I was starving. Then why had this happened? I put my hand on the clock. Its steady tick was comforting.

"We're waiting for you," Sally said crossly.

I pushed past Sally through the swinging door and took my place at the kitchen table.

"I've got to start cooking again," Mom was saying, eyeing the sandwich platter.

I reached for the salad. I'd been trying to lose a few pounds before school started, but it wasn't easy. I hadn't been able to convince my body it could do on less. I was always hungry.

"I wonder if your mother remembers how to fry chicken?" Dad asked, winking at me.

"What do you mean, Carl Morgan?" Mom flared. "Listen, I'm a good cook. I've been busy, remember?"

Dad threw up a hand. "Hey, don't I know? That's why I've decided we all need a break. You and Sally both have tomorrow off. Why don't we do something together? I'm thinking about a picnic."

"Oh, Carl, I'd like that," Mom exclaimed. "I suppose that means I'll have to fry chicken for it?"

Dad just grinned at her. The twins got the giggles and began punching each other on the arm.

"I'd rather go shopping," Sally said, looking down her nose.

I realized I'd eaten half a sandwich without even tasting it. I started on the other half, worrying about having seen that girl in the mirror. When she was in our backyard, she looked real enough. But did real people look back at you from a mirror? I had to have imagined it, I thought with a shudder.

"Jenny?" Mom said. I jumped. Everybody was looking at me. "I asked you if you think the picnic's a good idea," she went on. "I see that you weren't listening." She had that funny look on her face again.

"Earth calling Jenny," Sally groaned.

"I'm getting really bored with that, you know?" I snapped.

"Girls," Dad said patiently. "We're talking about a family outing. Can you hold down the bloodshed for right now?"

"Sure, Dad," I muttered. I tried not to reach for the potato chips, but I did. I got another sandwich, too. Well, salads don't fill me up, I argued in my mind.

"I thought you were dieting," Sally said, with a pointed look at my plate.

"I'm a growing girl," I told her.

And then it hit me. The first time I'd seen that girl in the yard, I hadn't eaten all day. The next time I saw her, I'd only had a piece of cake. I'd been dieting for days now, and today I saw her in my mirror. It must mean something.

I began to put it together. Mom could have

been right about my fainting the first time I saw the girl. Mom had said it was caused from hunger. Maybe that was the answer. If I got really hungry, strange things happened. I must have some weird kind of body chemistry, I thought.

That settled it. I couldn't afford to worry about my hips. If that's what it took to keep from seeing things, I'd better eat.

"Is the pie all gone?" I asked.

"That was yesterday," Mom said. "How about some cookies?"

I took a handful of cookies, feeling better already.

* * * * *

Mom and Dad let me stay up late to watch the movie. Nobody else liked westerns, so I had the TV all to myself. I had to promise to get up early the next day, though. Like Dad said, it wouldn't be any fun for Mom if she had to do all the work getting ready for the picnic.

Everybody else went to bed as usual. I got a cola and hunted for the chips, but they were all gone. I found the cookies instead and curled up on the floor to enjoy the movie. By the time the good guys won, I was stuffed.

I flipped off the set, turned out the lights,

and yawned my way upstairs. I was really tired. It was nearly midnight. I fell asleep as soon as my head hit the pillow.

Something woke me up—a car door closing, maybe. I peered at my watch in the moonlight. It was just after two. A gentle breeze moved my curtains. I lay watching them blow in and then flatten back against the screens. After a while I got up and pushed the curtains apart, so the air could move through the room better.

I leaned against the windowsill, looking out across the backyard. There was a car parked in the alley. That was funny. I couldn't see the car very well. The moonlight threw a black shadow from the tree across it. Who would park in the alley? I wondered.

I heard a noise downstairs, and froze. It sounded like someone was in the house. I slipped to the head of the stairs and looked down over the railing. There was a light down there. The light moved, and a board squeaked. Then I heard something screech—slowly, like a drawer being opened very carefully.

I went into Mom and Dad's room fast. I shook Mom.

"What is it?" Mom mumbled, her voice blurred. Then she saw me. "Jenny?"

"Listen, there's somebody downstairs," I

whispered. "I saw a flashlight."

Mom stared at me. Then she got out of bed in a hurry. "Don't wake Dad," she said softly. She grabbed her robe and pulled the bedroom door shut behind us. Then she started through the hall, flipping light switches on as she went. She turned on the upstairs hall light, then the one in the lower hall. She went through the living room and on into the kitchen. I was right behind her.

"There's nobody down here," Mom said at last. We'd been through all the rooms. Everything looked like we'd left it. Nothing seemed disturbed.

"Mom, I know I heard somebody," I said, puzzled. Then I looked past Mom's shoulder at the back door. "The door's open," I gasped.

Mom went to close it. "Didn't you check the doors before you came up to bed?" she asked crossly.

I had to admit I hadn't. "But Dad always does that," I argued. "You know he always locks up."

"Well, this time he didn't," Mom said. She started to turn off the lights. "Jenny, nothing's been bothered here. See? I think you dreamed it."

"Mom, I didn't dream it," I insisted.

"Jen. It's past two. Go to bed," she sighed.

"I heard somebody down here," I repeated, following her upstairs. "I didn't imagine it, Mom."

Mom put her finger to her lips and gently pushed me toward my room. I heard her settle back into bed. I walked to the window and looked out.

The car in the alley was gone. I got into bed and pulled the sheet up around my neck, shivering. I knew I'd been right, even if Mom didn't believe me. But what I didn't know was why someone would prowl around in our house.

Thunder began to rumble in the distance. I watched the lightning play across the sky. Then the rain began.

Seven

I guess I was too tired from being up late to go to sleep right away. I heard the clock strike four before I finally fell asleep. And then I wished I hadn't fallen asleep at all. Staying awake would have been better than the dream I had.

I dreamed of rushing water with a wooden bridge over it. I was wearing a long dress, and I was holding the hand of a child I didn't know. It was a boy wearing a round-brimmed hat. He looked up at me, laughing. I smiled, pointing out a butterfly near the edge of the stream.

The boy pulled his hand out of mine. He darted after the pretty butterfly. I called after him, but he didn't stop.

Then everything went into slow motion, like a film running down. I saw the boy teetering on the edge of the water. He was reaching for the butterfly. Then I saw his shoe slipping slowly off a mossy rock. I leaned toward him from the bridge, reaching. His wide eyes looked into mine as he fell silently into the raging water. His hat followed him down so slowly that it seemed to hang in the air for a long moment.

"No-o-o," I screamed, still reaching. My hand couldn't reach his. I heard the scream echo. *No-o-o . . . No-o-o . . .*

I sat straight up in bed, wide awake. My heart was pounding like I'd been running. It was the scariest dream I'd ever had, and I was glad to be awake.

I shivered, wondering where the dream had come from. It wasn't anything like the movie I'd watched the night before. I got up and started pulling my clothes out of the wardrobe, trying not to think about it.

"Jenny? You've got work to do," Sally shouted. "Come on. Mom wants you." Feet pounded up the stairs as I threw on my shorts and a cotton shirt. I stuffed my feet into my sneakers.

Sally stuck her head into my room. "You have to do the dishes," she said.

"Why me?"

"Hey, I made potato salad," Sally said indignantly. "I have to do something with my hair. Hurry up, will you?"

"You have to fix your hair for a picnic?" I groaned. But she'd already disappeared.

I brushed my hair and hurried down to the kitchen. Mom was packing fried chicken into a box. I reached for a leg, but she smacked my hand. "The cereal's on the table," she said briskly. "You didn't see any more prowlers last night, did you? I'm not telling Dad about that. There's no point in worrying him."

"Mom, I swear somebody was here," I insisted. "Listen, there was a car parked out back in the alley. Honest. The prowler probably got away in it."

Dad appeared at the back door. "Say, aren't we about ready?" he complained. "I can't hold the boys off much longer."

Mom began counting out forks and spoons. "Jenny, see what you can do about cleaning up the kitchen," she said, distracted. "Carl, can you put the chicken in the cooler?"

I started dumping dirty dishes in the sink. It looked like the subject of the prowler was closed. I wasn't surprised. That seemed to happen to me all the time.

* * * * *

It was hot and sunny, just right for a picnic. When we stopped to buy a watermelon on our way out of town, it felt like old times. We found a parking place right by the picnic area, even though the state park was really crowded. It was going to be a great day. I was sure of it.

We piled out of the car and claimed a picnic table while there were still a few left. Dad rolled the melon into the edge of the nearby creek to cool it. He and Mom sat down to watch the water. Sally and Daniel and I went off to explore. David stayed to play on the swings by the creek.

The park had a pioneer village with rebuilt log cabins you could go inside. Some were shops fixed up just as they'd been a long time ago. There were a lot of tourists on the paths and in the buildings.

For once, Sally forgot to be Miss Snooty. I couldn't believe it. She giggled and talked to me like she used to before she got into high school. It didn't last long, though . . . only until she spotted Jim Grover.

Jim drove slowly across the low bridge, looking around. Sally smoothed her hair back and waved at him. He stopped the car.

"What's he doing here?" I asked, suspicious.

"How would I know?" Sally said haughtily. "Hi, Jim!" she called.

"Yeah, hi, Jim," I grumbled. "You told him we were coming here, didn't you?"

Sally's eyebrows went up. "Why would I do a thing like that?" she asked sweetly. Jim had gotten out of his car and was coming toward us.

"This was supposed to be a family outing," I told Sally. "You had to go and spoil it. Come on, Daniel," I cried angrily. "Let's go see the mill. Sally doesn't need us. Do you, Sally?"

I didn't expect an answer. I dragged Daniel along behind me. My eyes were hot with tears. We crossed the wooden bridge and headed toward the old waterwheel at the mill.

"Darn that Sally!" I muttered. "Darn her, anyway."

"What's the matter?" Daniel asked, worried. "Are you mad, Jenny?"

I didn't answer. I just kept going. We were halfway to the mill when I heard Mom scream.

I dropped Daniel's hand and ran back toward the bridge. Mom screamed again. People were stopping to stare in her direction. She was running along the creek bank with Dad stumbling behind her. Then I saw what had happened. David was in the water. The thunderstorm the night before had swelled the rocky creek. The water was moving so fast that it tumbled David over and over as it carried him along.

"David!" I shouted, running as hard as I

could. I had to get to the wooden bridge before David was swept under it. I had to catch him. I pushed a man out of the way.

I threw myself flat on the floor of the bridge, hooking a leg around a post. I'd only have one chance to catch him. I knew the water was deep further on. He could drown.

Someone hit the planks beside me. It was Jim Grover. There was no time to think. The water threw David toward me. I reached for him at the same time Jim did.

We caught him. We dragged David up onto the bridge beside us, sopping wet and coughing. He began to cry, and so did I. I was shaking all over.

Jim was rubbing David's arms and legs when Mom got there. She fell to her knees and grabbed David. Then Sally was there, too. Jim started moving people back. I hadn't even seen the crowd until then.

My shoulder hurt. I kept holding it. "Dad!" I gasped, realizing suddenly that he wasn't with us. "Mom? Where's Dad?" I fought to my feet and pushed my way through the crowd. Dad was sitting on the ground fifty feet away. I ran to him. He was white as chalk.

"David?" he managed to say.

"We got him. He's okay," I told him in a rush. Then Mom was there beside me. She checked Dad's pulse and threw me a worried look.

"Carrie . . . ," Dad said, "short of . . . breath."

"I know," Mom said. "Jenny, put the food back in the car."

"I'm all right," Dad protested. "Are . . . you sure David's okay?"

"Look for yourself," Mom told him. Jim and Sally were coming across the grass, each with a twin.

"Jenny, we're going to the hospital," Mom said. "I want Dad and David checked over."

Dad protested, but Mom was firm. I agreed with her. Dad's color didn't look at all good to me. And when David got close enough to see, I was startled. He was breaking out in lumps all over. His arms were covered with them, and one eye was starting to swell shut. He was scared and shivering, too.

"What's wrong with David?" I cried.

"He ran into a swarm of hornets," Mom said briefly. "That's why he jumped into the water." She helped Dad to the car. Jim and Sally were putting the cooler in the trunk.

I stared after Mom and Dad. "Hornets? But . . . " Then I knew why that had surprised me. I'd expected Mom to say David had been chasing a butterfly. It was the dream. That's

67

how I'd known to lie flat to catch David instead of reaching over the railing.

"I must have ESP," I said blankly.

"Jenny?" Sally was running back toward me from the car. Everybody else was in the car. Jim Grover was leaning down, talking to Mom through the window.

"Listen, Jen," Sally said breathlessly. "I'm going to ride back with Jim. We'll meet you at the hospital."

"What?" I rubbed my shoulder. It really hurt now, and my hand felt funny. It was numb, and yet it tingled.

"Hurry, Jenny," Sally said impatiently. Mom honked the horn, waving at me.

I started for the car. "Ouch!" I cried, wincing. I stopped and looked at my leg. It was bright red in spots. I knew I'd have a big blue bruise on my calf and another on my thigh. It had happened when I hooked my leg around the post on the bridge, but I didn't care. David was okay . . . not like the boy in my dream.

"Jenny!" Mom shouted.

"Yeah, yeah," I shouted back, limping as fast as I could. David was alive. But Dad could have another heart attack, and I was wasting time.

"Hurry, Mom. Let's get to the hospital." I threw myself into the car.

68

We were moving before I finished saying it. I huddled in the corner of the backseat, thinking. I was trying to figure out why I'd had that dream. It felt like I'd had a warning. It was as if someone—or something—had wanted me to know what would happen at the park. If I hadn't had the dream, I might have stood there and watched David drown. I knew it was just one more thing I couldn't talk about. Who would believe such a crazy thing?

"Jenny, are you okay?" Mom asked. She peered at me in the rearview mirror.

I met her eyes. "Sure. I'm fine, Mom," I said. "Just drive, all right?"

Eight

WE must have been in the emergency room for hours. It felt like it, anyway. I was really relieved when the doctor said Dad was okay. I was a little upset that our day had been ruined. We used to have great picnics. But this one had been a disaster. I pushed the dream and the reason for it to the back of my mind. Since I couldn't explain it, I was hoping I could just forget it.

"We have all that food in the car and no place to eat it," I grumbled as we went down the walk to the hospital parking lot.

David scowled with one side of his face. The other side was too puffy for a scowl to work. "I'm not ever going back to that park," he said stubbornly. "I'm not going to get stung any more."

"I can't wear this sling to the pool," I said to anybody who wanted to listen. "I'm going to

70

get rid of the silly thing right now."

"Oh, honey, don't do that," Sally said. Jim looked at her with admiration. I couldn't stand it.

"Since when do you call me honey?" I snapped, looking for the fastener at the shoulder. "Listen, my X rays were normal."

"Jenny, your shoulder is not normal," Mom insisted. "It may not be broken, but you know the doctor told you it was badly sprained. You must keep that sling on."

"I'm really going to look sharp in a bathing suit," I shot back as I crawled into the car. "Come on, Mom."

"I'm hungry for chicken," David whined.

"We could picnic in our backyard," Daniel offered hopefully.

"We could go to the town park where the pool is," Mom said. "I've heard a lot of people use it. What do you think, Carl? Do you feel up to it?"

Dad waved his hand. "Hey, you heard the doctor. I'm in good shape."

Mom wavered. "All right, we'll do that," she said at last. "Would you join us, Jim? If you hadn't been there when you were, I don't know if Jenny could have held on to David. We can't thank you enough."

Sally blushed, and I stared at her. Some

family picnic, I thought. Then I felt bad for thinking it. I guessed Jim was okay. It was just that Sally was so different around him. It was like I didn't even have a sister anymore. She watched him all the time and acted all nervous and weird. I was surprised Mom didn't say something to Sally about it. If it had been me instead of Sally, I'll bet she'd have had something to say about it.

The town park was all lit up. I'd never been there in the evening. It was as crowded as it usually was during the day. A softball game was going on, and there were people watching the kids swim in the pool. Some of the people came over to talk to Mom and Dad. Everybody wanted to talk about David's narrow escape. I couldn't believe it. I asked Mom how they all knew about it so soon?

"That's the way small towns are," Mom told me, turning to greet yet another couple.

I didn't feel like talking, so I didn't. My shoulder hurt, and it was no fun eating chicken one-handed. Sally's potato salad wasn't as good as Mom's, but Jim Grover liked it. At least he ate enough of it after he found out Sally had made it.

Paul spotted his brother and came over to our table. He looked like he'd been swimming again. His hair was wet and slicked back.

"Hey, you're a real hero or something," he said excited. "How does it feel?"

"Listen, do you mind?" I told him. "It's all over, okay?"

"You don't have to bite my head off," Paul said, turning so red that his freckles stood out like paint spots.

I tried to think of something to say so he'd know I wasn't mad at him. "Do you swim all the time?" I asked. "No wonder you're such a good swimmer."

"Yeah, sure," Paul said, walking away. I saw him catch up to a group of kids and start talking to them. I could hear them laughing. I hoped they weren't laughing at me.

"Can we go home now, Mom?" I asked. "Please? I really don't feel very well."

Mom gave me an understanding look and signaled Dad. I wasn't sorry to leave. I'd told Mom the truth. I had a bad feeling in my stomach. I felt uneasy, like something awful was going to happen. Maybe it was because I'd been so scared about David. I just wanted to be safely home in my own room.

It was dark when we finished packing up the leftovers. By the time we got home, it had started to drizzle rain. It will be a good night to sleep, I thought, lifting my hot face to catch the cool mist. Dad went ahead to unlock the door. He stepped inside and turned on the lights.

"What's this mess?" he cried. He sounded angry. We crowded in after him and saw what he meant. There were pictures and frames all over the floor in the living room. Somebody had been in our house again. Bits of torn cardboard and paper were everywhere. There was a pile of broken glass by the couch.

"I guess the prowler came back," I said before I thought.

"What? What prowler?" Dad demanded, straightening up with a picture frame in his hand.

Mom and I looked at each other. "Carl," Mom said very carefully, "Jenny thought someone was in here last night."

"And you didn't tell me?" Dad flared. "Carrie . . ."

"We didn't want to worry you, Carl," Mom insisted. "Nothing was disturbed."

"The back door was open, though," I added. "Well, it was," I told Mom when she frowned at me.

"I didn't think anyone had been here," Mom explained. "I thought you just hadn't locked the door."

"I always lock the door," Dad said, his voice rising. "Carrie, I need to know these things.

Don't protect me, for Pete's sake. I'm not exactly an invalid." He and Mom weren't looking at each other. They were just talking at each other. It looked like there was going to be a big fight.

I took a deep breath and looked at Sally. "Should we call the police?" I asked brightly.

"Good idea," Sally said quickly. "I'll do that." She rushed into the hall and began to dial the emergency number.

Dad kicked paper aside and bent to examine the pictures. "Who would do a thing like this?" he asked.

Then I noticed that Dad's watercolors were still on the walls. "Dad," I began, "the pictures on the floor are the ones that were here when we moved in. They're the old family portraits. Maybe . . . "

Dad didn't hear me. "If Uncle Henry's photograph's been ruined, I'll . . . " He picked up another frame. "The back's gone, but the photo hasn't been torn," he said, relieved. Mom knelt beside him and began to pick up broken glass.

"Leave that alone, Mom," Sally cried, running into the room. "The police said not to touch anything."

"Dad," I tried again, "listen to me for a minute. Why didn't the crook tear up your

75

watercolors? Isn't that important?"

"What?" Dad asked, pulling the twins away from a pile of frames. "Don't bother this stuff," he told them. "The police need to see it."

"Boys, go to the kitchen," Mom said. "Sally, go with them. Get them some ice cream, and keep them in there."

"Why can't Jenny do that?" Sally grumbled, pushing the twins through the dining room. "I'll miss the police and everything." The kitchen door swung shut on her voice.

I was suddenly dizzy. I limped over to Dad's big chair and sat down. The room seemed to tilt and then level out. I held on to one arm of the chair to steady myself.

The police came right away. Mom and Dad both went to the door. A round-faced man— Officer Robertson, I heard him say—followed them into the living room. The officer let out a low whistle when he looked around.

"Do you folks have anybody mad at you?" he asked, writing something down in a long black notebook.

Dad looked astonished at the question. "Of course not."

"Well." The policeman tipped his cap back on his head. "Is anything missing?"

"We haven't looked," Mom admitted. "We

just got home, Officer Robertson."

"I'll take a look around outside, but I didn't see any broken windows," the officer said. "Are you sure the house was locked?"

"I used my key to get in," Dad told him, beginning to look annoyed. "See here, Officer . . ."

"Does anyone else have a key?" the man broke in.

Dad looked at Mom. "Just my wife. What are you getting at?"

"Somebody else has a key. Somebody we don't know about," I said loudly. "Isn't that what he means?"

The policeman shrugged. "Your daughter's got a point," he said. "I don't think this was a break-in. We haven't had one of those in this town in ten years."

I didn't want to hear any more. The police wouldn't find out who did this. This officer, at least, wasn't interested. He thought it was just a prank. That made me angry. A good detective would have noticed that the only pictures damaged were the old portraits. It had to mean something, but what?

"I'd change the locks," the officer told Mom and Dad when he left twenty minutes later. He had checked the house. There was no sign that anyone had broken in. "It looks like simple vandalism to me."

"We forgot to tell him about last night," Mom said after the policeman left.

"It wouldn't have changed his mind," Dad told her. "I'll see about changing the locks like he suggested. We don't know who Uncle Henry may have given a key to." He took a deep, shaky breath and leaned against the wall.

"Sally, bring the boys, and come in here," Mom called. I saw her shoot a worried glance at Dad.

"Stop that, Carrie," Dad said sharply. "I told you I'm not an invalid." He looked angry.

Somehow we all got upstairs. I found myself in my bed, too tired to remember undressing. I pushed my pillow around trying to make my shoulder comfortable. It throbbed like a toothache. When I closed my eyes, I kept seeing Mr. Fox. The lawyer's narrow face burned against the darkness. I couldn't make it go away.

It had begun to rain hard. The wind rattled the windows. The old house creaked and groaned as if it were alive . . . as if it had tightened to brace against the battering wind. I could almost hear the house breathe, deep and strong.

I sighed. I was cold, so cold. At last I fell into feverish sleep.

Nine

I slept fitfully through the night. Once I woke to hear Mom murmuring in the other room, and Dad's deeper voice answering. The sound was comforting, but it didn't stop the dreams.

My dreams were strange that night. Nothing fit together to make any sense. I dreamed something valuable was lost. I tried and tried, but I couldn't find it. Then I dreamed Dad was standing by my bed. He told me Uncle Henry's letter was missing. He couldn't remember the riddle, he said. *Behind the face the treasure lies,* I told him. But he was gone. Mr. Fox was there instead. The lawyer's eyes glittered. They glowed red, the way a wild animal's eyes do in a car's headlights. *You have the key,* he whispered. *No,* I said. *Go away,* I shouted.

"Jenny, hush." Mom was shaking my foot to wake me. "You were dreaming. How do you feel? How's your shoulder?"

It was morning. The sunlight streamed brightly through my windows. I touched my shoulder and cried out. "It's pretty sore," I mumbled.

"You had a hard day yesterday," Mom said. "Do you feel like breakfast now?"

I struggled to sit up in bed. The covers were wound around me as if I'd been fighting them all night. "Breakfast?"

Mom's brows came together to make a level line. "Jen, you're flushed." She put a cool hand on my forehead. Then she left the room. She came back with the thermometer and popped it into my mouth.

Mom left the room again and reappeared moments later. "One hundred and two," she said, shaking down the thermometer. "You must have the flu."

"Wonderful. Is that why I hurt all over?" I groaned.

"That's part of it. You stay right here," Mom ordered. I heard her run down the stairs.

I was freezing again. I tugged the quilt up around my ears. By the time I'd quit shaking, I was asleep.

A little later Mom came back. "Here," she said. "I've called the doctor. Take these."

I fought to open my eyes. I reached for the

tablets and swallowed them with what tasted like orange juice.

"I'm going to the drugstore for your prescription now," Mom told me. "There's toast on the tray. Try to rest." I felt her hand on my forehead again.

"Sure. Okay, Mom," I said. I really felt rotten. I began to cough. Why did I have to catch the flu? I already had a sprained shoulder. Wasn't that enough? I felt like crying, but it wouldn't have helped.

"It's not fair," I said. I pushed myself up and looked around. The tray was on the table by my blue pitcher, and Mom was gone again. She'd opened my windows, though. I could hear the twins outside, shouting at the dog next door.

I got out of bed and limped into the bathroom. I looked at myself in the mirror and brushed my teeth. I look crummy, I thought.

"Well, I feel crummy," I told myself as I crept back into my room. I crawled into bed. There wasn't anything else to do, so I went back to sleep.

"Jenny?" It was Sally. It began to look as if nobody in the family was going to let me sleep like I was supposed to. "I brought you a sandwich and a cola," she said, ignoring my scowl. "How are you feeling? Oh, here. Mom said to take this." She handed me a couple of capsules.

"What time is it?" I asked, reaching for the glass.

"I'm on my lunch break," Sally said. "Listen, you'd better not give me the flu. I can't miss work."

"How unselfish," I muttered.

Sally pushed a rose aside to look into my pitcher. "The water's almost gone," she remarked. "I'll fill it for you." She grabbed up the pitcher and started for the bathroom.

Then I heard a choked sound. It was Sally.

But that wasn't the worst of it. There was somebody laughing in my room. And it wasn't me.

I scrambled out of bed. I fell getting into the hall. I pulled myself back up, holding onto the door frame. Sally was in the bathroom staring at the pitcher in her hands. Her face was white.

I caught the pitcher just as she dropped it. What used to be roses was a mass of slime. I sat down hard on the edge of the tub.

Sally washed her hands over and over. "You think that's funny, don't you?" she cried.

I looked up at Sally and back at my pitcher. I began to shake. "Listen. Did you hear somebody laughing just now, Sally?"

"If anybody here is laughing, it's you," Sally shot back. "If you weren't sick, I'd . . . Oh!" She dried her hands and stalked out of the bathroom. "I'm going back to work," she said.

I'm hearing things again. What's wrong with me? I wondered. I got up slowly and dumped the slimy mess into the wastebasket. Then I rinsed the pitcher and took it back to my room.

I was too tired to think, and I was burning up. I started coughing. I knew I was really sick. Maybe the fever had made me hear that laughter. Anyway, my room was quiet now. I crawled back into bed. The pillow was cool on my cheek. I drifted into sleep.

The day was endless. I ached all over, and people kept waking me up to give me pills. Once I saw the twins staring at me from the hall. Dad took them back downstairs. Then Mom was there dressed for work in her white uniform. She looked worried. I tried to smile at her and went back to sleep. When I woke again, she was gone. My supper tray sat on my table, untouched.

That odd little tune I'd almost forgotten about kept coming back. I'd wake, and it would just be fading away. I kept trying, but I couldn't quite remember how it went. There was a sharp pain in my chest. The furniture in my room looked blurry. I heard Dad put the twins to bed and turned my head to look out the window. There was one star. A dark cloud passed over the moon as I watched. I wondered if it would rain again.

I dreamed someone was humming that tune. It might have been me. I opened my eyes to see the moon high and white in the sky. There were no clouds. The pain in my chest was worse than the one in my shoulder now. It hurt to breathe. I heard the clock downstairs strike two. The sound was dim. I moaned and rolled over.

I saw a girl sitting in the corner in a pool of moonlight. Her rocking chair moved gently back and forth. I wondered where the chair had come from. She was sewing. I could see the glint of the needle in her hand. I knew now who had been humming that song. The sound was loud in my room. And then it stopped. Thick silence pulsed in my ears. My room might have been on an island, far from shore.

My voice came out in a hoarse whisper. "How long have you been here?" I asked.

The girl smiled. Moonlight touched her braided hair and lay across her shoulder. I could see the high neckline of her long dress. I knew her. It was the girl in the mirror. She reached to put her sewing on my table, and I saw the ruffle at her elbow fall back.

"What do you want here? Did you spoil my flowers?" I asked.

The girl didn't answer. I couldn't tell if she'd even heard me. She stood up and touched the frame of my mirror. Then she turned her face toward me.

"I know. I saw you in the mirror. But what do you want?" I repeated. "Won't you talk to me?"

The figure touched the mirror again. Her head tilted as if she were listening to something. Then she passed into the hall without a sound.

"Wait," I cried. "Don't go." I flung the covers back and struggled to my feet. I followed her into the hall. She stood at the head of the stairs, looking down. She seemed to glow. It must have been a trick of the moonlight. The house was caught up in that deep silence. I could hear nothing but my ragged breathing. I clutched at the pain in my chest and walked toward the girl.

"Please talk to me," I begged. If she would only speak, I knew she could tell me what had been happening to me. I had to know.

The girl lifted her head. She glided slowly down the stairs as if I hadn't spoken. I crept after her, holding tight to the railing. The stairs were dark, and I was panting. I stopped on the landing to catch my breath. I looked out the oval window into the moonlight.

The yard was lit as bright as day. The bushes threw sharp shadows across the grass. That car was in the alley again. I gasped and jerked back, away from the window. My heart began to pound. Should I call Mom? I wondered.

The girl stood at the bottom of the stairs, waiting for me. Before I could decide what to do, I found myself walking down the stairs. One, two, three . . . ten steps and I was in the downstairs hall.

The girl had disappeared. Dazed, I clung to the stair post. The hall was black except for patches of moonlight, and I was alone. I heard a car drive slowly down the alley.

Sounds came from the dining room. There was a scratching noise and then a muffled clunk. I stiffened. Someone was in the house—someone who had no right to be there. Suddenly I was angrier than I'd ever been before.

I walked steadily through the dark living room and stopped in the wide doorway. A flashlight lay on the table. Its beam was almost hidden by the figure bending over it. I heard the crack of thin glass breaking and reached out to flip on the light.

A man whirled to face me. He was dressed in black. All I could see were his eyes. They gleamed black between his pulled-down cap and the turtle-neck he'd drawn up to cover his nose and mouth. He snarled and lunged at me. He knocked me aside, turning off the light switch at the same time. I cried out as I fell.

I heard a scratching noise. I looked up to see the prowler snatching something up from the table. I screamed as he turned back to me. His arm was raised. He was going to hit me with his flashlight.

The room lit up in a vivid gleam of blue light. The prowler's arm dropped. He backed away, but he wasn't looking at me. His eyes were wide, and they were fixed at a point behind me. He made a sound, a kind of gurgle. Then he ran to put the table between himself and whatever he saw. The curtains billowed as if a strong wind were blowing them. I thought I saw the shining figure of a girl move past me toward the man.

The prowler shouted something and fell back toward a window. The glass shattered as he went through it. Upstairs there was another crash, and the twins began to scream.

I fainted.

Ten

MY head was in Sally's lap when I woke up. She kept rubbing my hands and asking what had happened. I didn't know what to tell her. I didn't understand what I'd seen. It had all happened so suddenly.

All the lights downstairs were on. I could hear Mom talking very fast on the phone in the hall. Daniel was looking at me and crying as hard as he could. I reached for him, and he threw himself on top of me.

"Ouch," I groaned. "Be careful, Daniel."

"Don't die, Jenny," Daniel sobbed. "Don't die."

"Don't be silly," I told him. "Do I sound like I'm dying? Hey, lighten up, okay?" My voice didn't sound exactly normal. But I guess Daniel believed me, because he quit crying. I pushed him off and managed to sit up. "The prowler fell through the window," I said.

"Somebody had better call the police, quick."

"I just did that," Mom cried. She ran toward me and grabbed me. "I'm so glad you're all right," she kept saying. "Why did you come down here alone?"

"But I wasn't alone," I managed to say against her shoulder. "At least, I don't think I was. Listen, they've got to catch him."

"It's all right now, Jen," Mom said. "We're here. They'll get him."

"They already did," Dad said. He was coming through the dining room.

"Oh, they couldn't have," Mom said, turning me loose. "I just now called, Carl. They haven't had time."

"Officer Robertson's been keeping an eye on the house," Dad told her. He looked grim. "He was patrolling the alley and saw the man fall through the window. By the time Fox got out of the bushes under the window, Robertson had him handcuffed. There's something wrong with Fox, though. He was spouting a pretty wild story.

"Fox?" Mom said sharply. "Do you mean Lawyer Fox?"

Dad nodded. "The same."

"But why?" Sally cried.

"That's what I'd like to know," Dad replied angrily. "And I'd like to know what he was

89

doing with our mantel clock, too." He picked up a wire coil from the dining table and threw it back down.

"Oh, my poor clock," I said, and burst into tears. "She didn't come soon enough," I cried, coughing.

"Who, Jen?" Mom asked, looking at me hard.

"The girl . . . you know, that girl. . . . She didn't come soon enough to save her clock."

Mom bit her lip. "She's delirious."

"No, she's not," Dad told her. "She's had a bad shock. I'd like to hit that lawyer."

"I think Jen's got pneumonia. She ought to be in the hospital," Mom said.

"Oh, not again," I protested, wiping my eyes. "I just want to go to bed, Mom. Please?"

"Why is everybody sitting on the floor?" David shouted, rushing into the living room. "Look what I found upstairs!"

"David, you need to be quiet," Mom said. "We have things to take care of here."

"Mom," David whined, "you have to look. See? Look what was sticking out of Jenny's mirror when it fell down. Can I have it? It's play money, Mom."

Dad took the handful of paper from David and looked at it. Then he sat down hard in his chair and blew out a long breath. "I don't believe it," he said shaking his head.

"What is it, Carl?" Mom picked up one of the sheets of paper to examine.

"Bearer bonds. These are bearer bonds," Dad said slowly. "No wonder Fox wanted to buy the house. That's what he was after. They're worth a lot of money. Uncle Henry must have bought them with the money he got when he sold off his land for building lots. I just supposed he'd given all the money away. He was like that."

"Who do they belong to now?" Sally asked.

"The owner of a bearer bond isn't listed anywhere," Dad explained. "Anyone who has them can cash them in. If Fox had found them, he could have exchanged them for money."

"And nobody would have ever known he'd stolen them," Mom said, looking shocked.

"Exactly," Dad agreed.

"We're rich," Sally cried. "Think of it, Jenny."

"There's more upstairs," David added. "I saw lots more of those things."

"I don't think I'd call it rich," Dad said. "But there should be enough to help out."

I didn't know why everybody was so excited. It was only money. "Mom, what about my mirror?" I asked. "It isn't broken, is it?"

Mom shook her head. "There's glass all over

your floor. I'm sorry, Jenny."

"Uncle Henry must have hidden the bonds under the wooden back of the mirror," Dad was saying.

"Behind the face the treasure lies," Mom said softly. "Oh, Carl. Mr. Fox sneaked in here and read Henry's letter. He must have. But he thought the treasure was hidden behind one of those old portraits. That's why he ripped them apart."

"And when it wasn't there, he thought it was behind the clock face," Dad said.

"The treasure was in Jenny's room all the time," Sally added. "Good grief! A fortune in that old mirror."

"I doubt if it's a fortune," Dad said dryly. "Don't start planning a trip to Paris yet, Sally."

"I'm really sorry about your mirror, Jenny," Mom said. "We can have a new mirror put in the frame, though. I can't imagine why it fell when it did," she went on, puzzled.

I knew, but I didn't say anything. The girl had made it fall, just like she had chased Mr. Fox out. It was almost too much to think about.

"Can we talk about all this later?" I asked. I was trembling. I still felt faint and kind of sick. "I want to go to bed, Mom."

"You'd better sleep in my room with me, honey," Sally said. She helped me to my feet, and I looked up at her, surprised. She really cared. I could tell.

"But . . . ," Mom began.

"She needs rest, Carrie. It's almost morning anyway," Dad told her.

I let Sally put me to bed in her room and tuck me in. It was funny how much she reminded me of Mom just then. My chest still hurt, but I felt somehow . . . peaceful. And I was awfully sleepy.

"See you in the morning, Jen," Sally said softly. "You call me if you need me."

"Yes. Thanks, Sally," I said "Sally?"

She turned back to my bed. "Yes?"

"Just . . . thanks."

Sally grinned. "You're okay, kid," she said.

* * * * *

Two months later, almost everything that had happened seemed like a dream. The bearer bonds were real, though. We had painted the house. We all had college funds now. Dad had fixed up the barn and gone into business for himself.

When I was finally well, it had been time for school to start. The twins really liked the new school, and so did I. Kim Blair didn't worry me anymore. Most of the kids were pretty nice.

I made new friends, too. I was in my room waiting for three of the girls to come by for me. We were going to the football game, and they were late.

I looked out my bedroom window for the fourth time. I rushed back to the mirror to work on my hair. I wanted it to be just right for the homecoming game. There was a junior high sock hop after the game. Paul had asked me if I were going. Maybe he'd ask me to dance. The thought made me nervous.

"I hate my hair," I groaned.

Sally was lounging on my bed writing a letter to Jim Grover. "Your hair looks fine," she told me. She put her pen down and got up to tie my ribbons for me. They were school colors, red and white.

"Sally, am I pretty?" I asked, studying myself in the mirror. "I'm serious."

Sally looked at me critically. "You'll do," she said, and went back to her letter.

Well, it was better than nothing. I fluffed out my hair, remembering when I'd seen the girl in the mirror. I touched the locket I was wearing. Dad had found it in the clock when he gathered up the pieces. It had been my great-grandmother's locket. There was a rose carved on the outside. And I had known before I'd opened it what would be on the inside. The girl in the mirror—the other Jenny—had smiled out at me from the small faded picture.

"The girls are here," Sally said. "I heard the back doorbell."

I grabbed my heavy sweater out of the wardrobe. "Are you sure you don't want to go with us?" I asked.

"Oh, I don't really like football," Sally said. "Besides, Tracy's coming over to help me with my science project."

I stopped in the doorway. Tracy Barnes was a brain. He was also tall, dark, and gorgeous. "Is Tracy why you don't like football any more?" I teased. "What about Jim?"

"What about him?" Sally replied. "He's a good friend, that's all."

"Oh," I said.

Sally looked up at me. "Listen, Jen. I'm not going to get serious about Tracy or Jim, at least not for a long time, okay? I've got to think about college next year. Things change."

Yes, I thought, things change. And many times they change for the better. I ran down the stairs. Our family was all together and happy. Dad was better, and I had new friends now. I didn't know how, but I knew the other Jenny had helped it all happen.

I hadn't seen her since the night Mr. Fox was caught. Nothing really strange had happened to me since then, either. My room was bright and cheerful and perfectly normal.

She was gone for good. I knew that because of the roses I'd found on my pillow the first day of school. That was six weeks ago. The roses still looked beautiful. Strong and fragrant, they bloomed in my blue pitcher as if they'd just been picked. . . .

They were a parting gift from a friend.